ISBN: 9798589301403

Cover design by: John Jones.
Library of Congress Control Number: 2018675309
Printed in the United States of America

The Girl Who Spoke to the Wind

The Girl who spoke to the Wind

By David Halpin.

Illustrations by

John Jones.

1.

The wind could not explain how it could see, but when it moved over fields and through the branches of trees it knew when to bend and fall, when to rush and suddenly drop before racing towards a soaring bird or skimming across the languid surface of a river.
Sometimes, if it tried hard enough, its vision was something that encompassed the entire world.
The wind carried the last breath of all creatures and never forgot where they had first come from. It held promises, kept and broken, within itself, and although some were whispered and others screamed, the wind heard them all. The wind knew the valleys and canyons of the world, from the faces of scabrous sun- burnt rock to the delicate fingers of hanging moss that sheltered within the cracks of secret mountain passes. It swept into cities, roared through forests of buildings, spinning rain onto the glass towers and down upon the people below.

Sometimes, it almost stopped entirely, moving only enough to touch a grain of white sand on a silent beach. At times like this the wind would almost remember, as if it was something more than it could understand and it would drift in slow circles before breaking free of its strange introspection.

Then, the wind would laugh again, and run towards the sky and the places it saw in the distance.
But the wind could still not explain how it could see.

2.

The house sat at the edge of a large forest. A small girl stumbled down the wooden porch steps and fell forward onto the damp grass. She sighed before struggling to her feet, unsure of whether to cry or not. Opening her fingers, she inspected the three pieces of bread that were now pressed together. She looked back towards the kitchen door where a young woman smiled and gestured the girl onwards.
The girl turned away and looked around her, in awe of the resounding bird call and wondrous noises that came from the woods. Finally, she pressed her lips together and strode forward and clumsily flung the pieces of bread into the air. She had turned and was already running back to the house before they landed on the grass.
She raced to the porch steps and immediately sat down, elbows on her knees and hands under her chin.

"Now, watch what happens," the woman whispered, sitting down beside her, "We have to stay quiet."

A whistle broke from the woods, something delicate and curious. A small brown bird fluttered above the pieces of bread, then darted back to its branch.

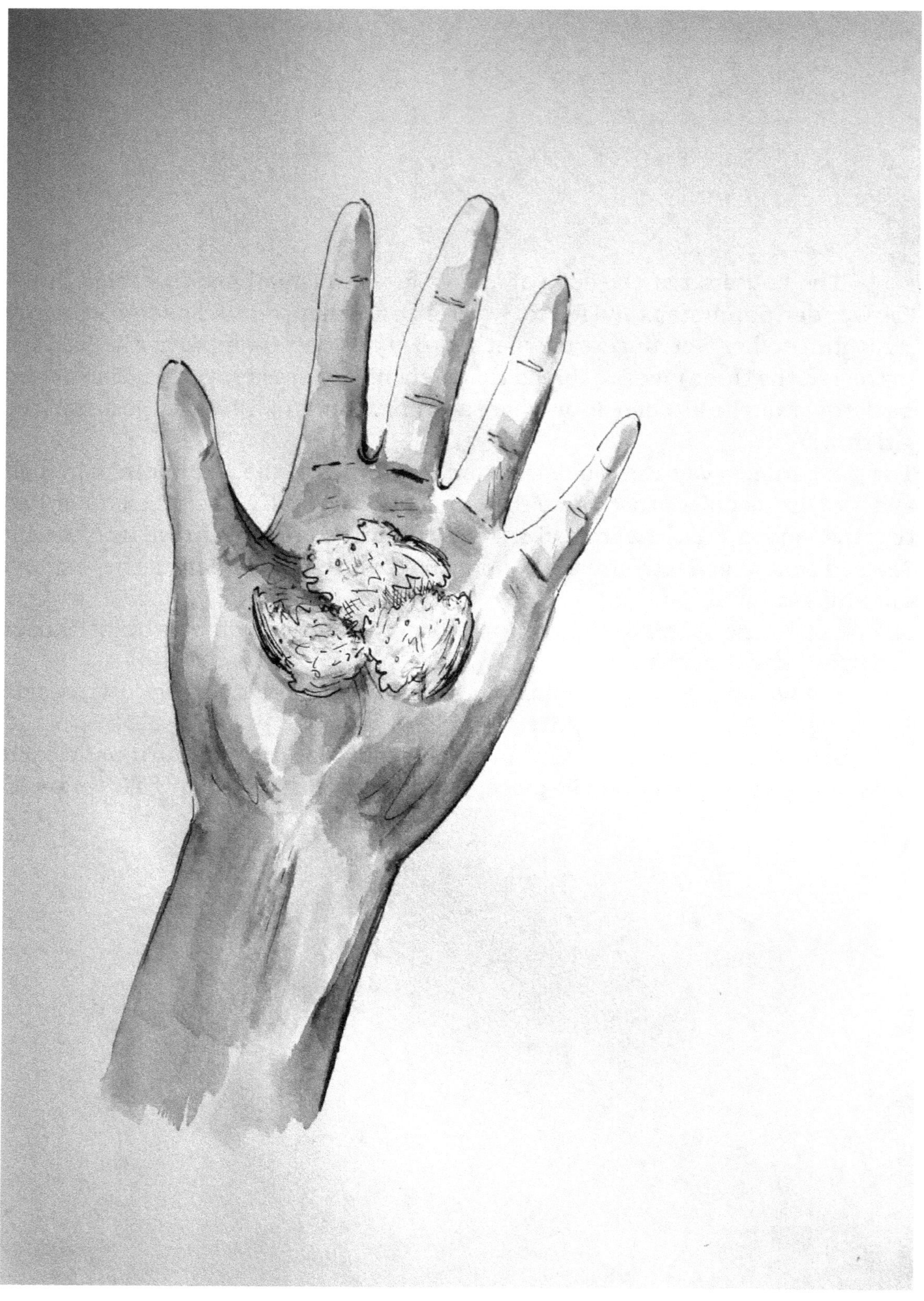

"He's making sure it's not a trick."

"Why?" the girl asked, "I'm not tricking. It's his breakfast!"

The woman smiled again, "Well, he has to check that there are no cats around before he lands."

"Oh."

The bird returned again, this time landing close to the bread. Its tiny head darted sided to side before it hopped forward and pecked at one of the pieces and flew away.

"Hooray!" the girl exclaimed, "He won't be hungry now."

She stood up and ran to the remaining pieces of bread, picked one up and tried to throw it nearer the trees but instead it landed behind her.

"It's alright, petal, the birds will find it."

"But the cat might come!" she answered.

"Not while we're keeping guard, don't worry."

The girl thought about this for a moment then decided her mother was right. She left the remaining piece of bread where it was and tip-toed back to the porch steps, imagining that there might be a fairy hiding beneath every blade of grass she stood on, like in her storybook, and she had to be careful to avoid stepping on them.

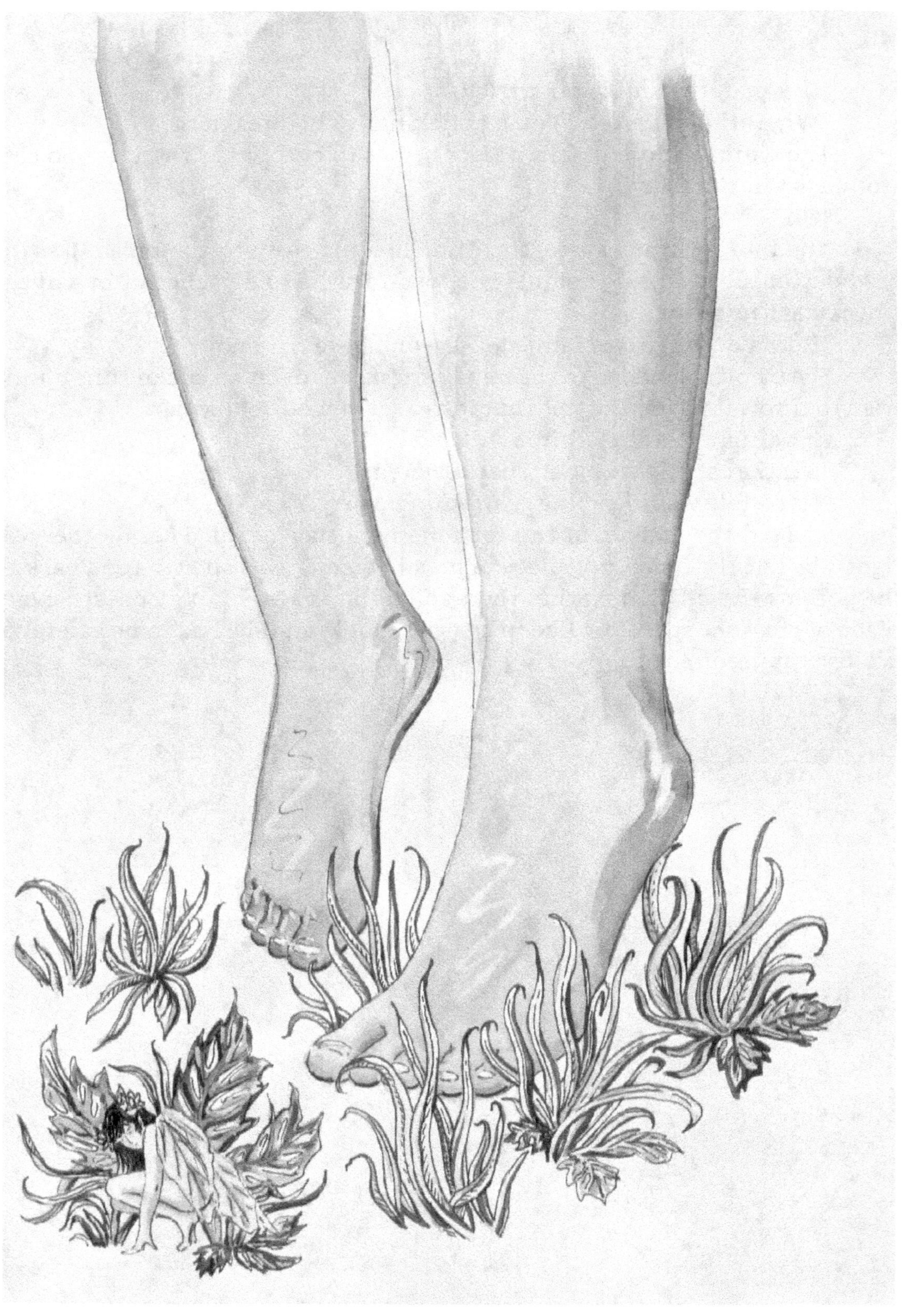

"Can we get some bread for the fairies too?"

"I don't think they'd like it," her mother answered, "And besides, they're all too full up after their party last night."

The girl was silent at this before her face slowly lit up.

"Were you at the party when I was asleep?"

"No. But I saw them from the window."

"Oh. Can I see them tonight if I'm good?"

"Well, maybe not those fairies, but if you are good, really good I mean, you might see the dream fairies instead."

"Ok. But I'm always good."

The woman eyed her daughter sceptically before smiling.

"Yes, you are…most of the time."

She shivered as a cold breeze appeared suddenly, sending a silver ripple through the swaying grass and rattling the crisp golden leaves that covered the looming trees.

"I think it's going to rain, we better go back inside."

The wind arched itself around the trees and turned back towards the house, tracing its weight across the grass and through the weathered wood of waving branches. It then coiled itself tightly and nudged one of the remaining pieces of bread that the girl had thrown. The sparrow chirped in protest, unable to reach the bread as the wind flexed itself and buffeted the small bird away. A twisting finger of air lifted the bread upwards and carried it to a nook in a nearby tree before allowing it to settle.

The sparrow immediately darted after the wind and hopped into the nook before pecking at the bread and carrying it away.

The wind circled again, this time scattering the crisp red leaves that carpeted the forest floor before rustling the matted black fur of the silent cat who had been about to pounce upon the sparrow. The wind laughed and its voice sang through the branches of the trees and whispered across the shale surface of the nearby riverbank.

From the window of the house the girl called out to her mother, pointing excitedly at the high place in the tree where she had seen the bread mysteriously rise to.

"It's only the wind." the girl's mother told her.

"But who is the wind?" the girl asked, pressing her face against the glass, "Who are you?" she called out.

The wind rattled the window frame in reply before rising further and higher until it was far away, the girl's words like musical notes in its mind until, somehow, it was far across the other side of the world.

But it couldn't forget the words of the girl.

Who am I? The wind whispered to itself, over and again. Who am I?

3.

The wind knew no sense of time and would feel surprise and even fury when it returned to a special place to find a favourite tree gone or a house demolished and long since abandoned. And because the wind would sometimes allow its thoughts to fall far into itself, it could travel for years without its memory surfacing, like a drifting sea without a centre, a body without a mind.

This was always a choice the wind made because of what it saw on its travels: a slow, numbing crawl across a battlefield where it would lightly touch the faces of dead soldiers in dismay, a mournful song though a dwindling string of starving families as they trekked through a scorched landscape without shelter from a baking sun.

Other times it was a child in a dark laneway, hunkered and broken, abandoned by the world. Sometimes the wind would rouse itself awake only to find itself above a once dense tropical forest, uprooted and stripped, the rich earth poisoned by chemicals and the pollutants of newly installed oil wells or mine drains.

These were some of the reasons why the wind hid away inside itself and these were also the reasons why it always felt the need to eventually come back.

Years passed, and the wind, when it returned to the house, discovered that the girl was now older and had become frail and thin. It found her sitting on a swing that faced the woods and it became curious, moving around her softly, stroking her pale face and flexing itself just enough so as to allow her to rock back and forward without having to push herself.

The door of the house opened and the woman peered outside, her hair now streaked with grey and her face strained and etched with a mask of concern. The wind moved closer, trying to understand.

"Oh, Jane, please come inside. It's getting cold. You need to stay warm.

The doctors..."

"I'm sick of what the doctors say," the girl murmured to herself. But the wind heard. It rose again and pulled warmth from one of its trails from a far away country, sending a sigh of summer upon the girls face. She looked around then, as if someone had whispered to her.

"I'm not cold. I'll go back inside in a while."

The girl's mother didn't answer. She watched her daughter on the swing and closed her eyes, as if making a wish. Then she closed the door.

How long have I been away, the wind wondered?

While the wind could remember all things it didn't have the kind of mind to place them in any order: a week or a century made no difference to the wind, and tomorrow was just a yesterday yet to arrive.

The girl carefully climbed off the swing and placed her arms around herself. She coughed for a long time and held herself rigid until she stopped, as if she was afraid something inside her might break. Finally, she sighed and walked slowly into the woods.

The wind rolled cautiously above her, unfolding as softly as it could across the tree tops, focusing itself into one point, before descending silently, like the tip of a snowflake, through the trees.

The wind knew instinctively that it was spring; vibrant grasses rang out shades of emerald, and red buds on trees were broken by the protrusion of new branches. Across the sky the wind felt birds beat freely and wheel without thought through the blue.

The girl was outside all of this. A black woollen hat and scarf drew the wind to the pale contours of her thin face and although she wore a long, dark coat, her shoulders poked through the material and the wind felt her frailty as it moved across her arms and back.

The girl walked further and further into the woods until it was difficult for the wind to follow her: the treetops encroached upon each other here, their high limbs entwined and it was difficult to see where one tree was separate from another.

The wind rose and circled the highest boughs causing the ancient wood to stretch and moan in its wake but it couldn't penetrate the canopy of woven branches. When the girl finally emerged from the trees the wind glanced softly against her face, drying the tear marks that the girl had missed before she returned to the house.

4.

In the weeks that followed, the wind learned to keep its distance from the girl in case she might succumb to her mother's protests.

It was always the same argument.

"I'm alright! It's not cold out."

"You can't afford to..."

"I can't afford to waste the rest of my life in a room!" the girl would cry, "Please, I just...I want to be outside. It's only for a little while."

So the wind would slowly tumble in wide circles around the property, combing itself in the fields of emerging grain, stretching across the back of the wide river and scratching on its sandy banks before fracturing its strength within the bloom of the vast wood's green treetops.

As the girl found it more and more difficult to make her way into the deepest parts of the woods, her mother would wheel her to the end of the garden and reluctantly leave her alone with a book. The wind would then allow itself to flow across the carpet of grass before curling around the girl, becoming a whisper through the pages before touching her fingers and face.

Sometimes, it seemed to the wind that the girl knew it was there; she would stare straight ahead as it brushed against her and half close her eyes, as if sensing its presence. She would then begin to say something before stopping herself, as if her imagination might be playing tricks on her.

So the wind decided it would speak first.

It allowed its mind to feel each tree close to the girl until it sensed a hollow it could glance against then it began to double back on itself until a sound began to call from the tree.

"Whooo...Whooo," the wind called, its voice a funnelled force of air ringing through the tree, "Whooo!"

"What?" the girl answered, peering into the woods, "Is somebody there?"

The wind wanted to ask if the girl knew its name, but no matter how it twisted and pushed, the only sound that it could make was the same word over and over.

"Whooo...Whooo!"

The girl was seventeen years old and had spent the last two years travelling from hospital to hospital, seeing doctors, radiologists and specialist oncologists who tried to support the straining ceiling of her world like narrow pillars. Her world wanted to stretch further and find more years but there were no more pillars to hold it up.

She became fascinated with the places and things that she would never see, absorbing the images of exotic lands in books that she would fixate upon over and over again.

Each time she had the strength to venture out to the garden she would carry a different book on her lap and she would read out the names of rare flowers and animals on the verge of extinction, shaping the words carefully as if some strange alchemy might assemble these things before her from the sounds she made.

"Zaglossus bartoni; the Eastern Long-beaked Echidna!"

She couldn't say why she spoke these things instead of just thinking about them, maybe it was because she never felt truly alone when she was in the garden; as if the fairies that she had believed in when she was younger were in fact real and watched her from the woods.

She would sometimes face down into the pages of her books but peer secretly into the cover of the trees just in case.

I'm retreating into my imagination because I don't want to face what's really happening, she would think then. She would remember everything about her illness and this time, when she stared, it was only into a world of her own, which was something frightening and stark where darkness waited upon the edges of all the moments she tried to keep for herself.

And yet, she did feel different in the garden even if her mother worried about her being outside. It was as if...what? *There is comfort here, she thought. The sounds of the woods seem to call to me and the wind seems warmer here than anywhere else. And something deeper too, though. Something stranger and more elusive than that; this place knows me.*

"Who are you?" She barely whispered the words, as if daring anyone or any thing to hear her.

"Whooo!" the wind replied, "Whooo!"

As the summer progressed the girl grew weaker and sat in the garden less and less. The wind would call for her, knocking against the windows of the house but this only had the effect of separating them further as the girls mother would, at the sound of the wind outside, pull the curtains and lock the doors. She would sometimes stare deep into the woods, as if she was aware that something strange was occurring but was unable to comprehend what it could be.

On the morning the girl was taken away, the wind had been tracing figure 8's around the property. The ambulance siren cut high and violently through the sky as it approached the house, startling the wind and sending birds, like thrown confetti, from the surrounding trees.

The girl's mother ran from the house, screaming at the two men in green uniforms who scrambled from the shrieking vehicle. Her face was flushed and streaked with tears as she dragged the first man into the house.

He emerged again almost immediately, bounding to the ambulance door and speaking urgently into his radio.

The wind rushed towards the house and exploded through the rooms until it found the girl. She was lying on the kitchen floor with a blanket over her body and an oxygen mask over her face.

"Shut the door, for God's sake!" the woman screamed.

"Try to stay calm," the man kneeling next to the girl replied, "We're going to move her now, alright? Do you have a medication diary?"

"But...the wind. It's too cold in here..."

The man took the woman's hand, "Don't worry about that. Now, do you have a diary, a list of taken medication and times? We need to see it before we..."

"Yes." the woman answered, "Yes, I'll...it's in the bedroom."

The wind stroked the girls face. It wanted to feel her breathing but the hard plastic of the mask prevented contact. The second man returned and shut the door and... the wind found itself back outside the house. It watched from the edge of the woods as the men emerged carrying the girl. She was wrapped in a red blanket and her mother was holding her hand and whispering to her, but the wind chose not to listen this time. It was afraid of what it would hear.

The wind raged and shook the world. It found the deepest ravines and spilled itself through them at dizzying speeds. It searched for the thickest and most dense forests and smashed itself against them, leaving a wake of impossible destruction and debris. And it sang out fearfully within long forgotten caves and caverns that stretched deep into the bowels of the earth, becoming a primal force again and almost forgetting the reason for its sorrow. Yet, somehow, when night fell, the wind found itself back outside the girl's house again.

The wind grazed the unlit windows and locked doors before rising onto the roof and carefully spiralling down the chimney. It stretched out across the darkness and whispered into the girl's bedroom.

The floor was littered with the signs of that morning's chaos: a broken glass, a spill of white tablets, crumpled sheets and a book that lay crookedly against the edge of her bed. The wind brushed against the open pages, noticing how the girl had circled one of the illustrations; Epiphyllum Oxypetalum: The Kadupul Flower.

The wind held within itself a memory of all the world's rarest things. It had been reminded of creatures and plants it had touched and caressed when it listened to the girl speak their names from the book and even the rare flower she had circled was something that the wind remembered from its many travels.

The Kadupul flower rarely bloomed, but when it did, it only occurred at midnight and would then wilt and die before dawn.

The wind called back through itself, feeling its many fingers all across the world. It searched for the flower through humid night-time mountains and damp, tropical glades. It caressed the fronds of secret, exotic plants and the petals of hidden blossoms until it discovered, high on a Sri Lankan hillside, a Kadupul flower just about to bloom.

The moonlight struck the flower's delicate pale lobes as if bestowing a clandestine kiss and the wind marvelled at this nocturnal embrace.

But, its thoughts quickly returned to the girl and it began to curl itself tightly around the stem, pulling the flower carefully from the moist, black soil. The wind twisted tightly, encapsulating the flower in a vortex of warm air that would keep it alive for as long as it took to bring the flower to the girl.

Then the wind rose. It lifted the flower above the canopy of treetops and pushed it through a channel of its whirling hands that carried the delicate cargo over oceans and continents at a speed that made the wind forget all other things in the world. The girl will see the flower and know, the wind thought to itself; she will know I am here and she will tell me who I am.

When the wind reached the shores of the girl's country it allowed itself a moment to linger upon all the scents and countless breaths of the land's creatures and people in order to find the girl. It exploded outward like a new nebula of currents, sending spindled draughts into the night, touching all things until it discovered her. When it finally did, the wind knew something terrible had happened.

The light from the room was stark and too sharp, cutting around the figures inside like a scissors.

The wind held itself against the glass and watched as the girl lay unmoving upon a small bed in a cramped room. Her mother was kneeling next to her with her head in the girls lap. The wind had been so concerned with carrying the flower that it had missed the girl's final breath. It pressed the flower against the hospital window, holding it there, not for anyone else to see but only to somehow show the girl that it had been thinking of her.

It drew a freezing breeze from one of its tails that rippled across a far and snowy northern land and blew it around the flower, frosting the glass and fusing the flower onto its surface. Then the wind fell away.

It didn't want to look back, but when it did the wind saw a silhouette of the girl's mother tracing the outline of the flower as she stood next to the hospital window and faced outward into the night.

DAVID HALPIN

5.

The wind could not explain how it could see, and it could not explain why it had loved the girl. Like all timeless mysteries and all great friendships, sometimes the reward is not an answer but the question itself. But the wind, flirtatious and erratic in its thinking, could never come to this conclusion for it was, in its true heart, no more than a child.

And so, finally, after many years wandering the world, the wind returned to the girl's house. It was an autumn evening with a sky that washed the dusk with red and purple blooms, and the first stars glistened as if grains of sand had been flung high above the sinking sun. The house was dark and unkempt and wild grass encroached almost to the porch steps. The wind glanced against the walls and windows but sensing no warmth from within, it turned upwards and began to climb. Then it heard a voice.

Descending gently, the wind saw a woman tentatively make her way out of the house and onto the porch. She leaned upon a wooden stick to support her thin frame.

"Is that you?" she said, facing the woods, "Are you back?"

The wind became flustered and keeled outwards, fanning the edge of the trees in panic; the woman was speaking to the wind! How did she know it could hear her, it wondered?

As if sensing the winds confusion, the woman spoke again.

"I don't know what you are, a ghost or..." she closed her eyes and sighed, "Or something else, but, I do know, somehow, you made my daughter happy. And I thank you for that."

The wind felt the impossible horizons of feelings it could never explain or comprehend emanate from inside itself and it tried to reply to the woman by glancing against the cracked and broken knots of the oldest trees but the only sound it could make was an unfocused whisper.

The woman's arm trembled as she leaned upon her walking stick.

"It's almost my own time now," she said, "I'm glad. I've had too many years without my daughter. I just want to see her again."

The wind curled in slow revolutions as the woman made her way back inside the house, her stick tapping the way before her as if affirming the reality of a world she didn't want to believe in anymore.

It was then that the wind realised that it could, in some way, give the woman what she wanted.

DAVID HALPIN

It poured itself across the ground, dragging leaves and broken branches into its embrace. It plucked twigs and moss from the forest carpet, combining everything into a crude caricature of a human being, assembling the body and twisting through its limbs, making it walk towards the house.

Dead grass mimicked the girl's hair, while mildew-spotted leaves folded over and upon each other, creating what the wind imagined would resemble the girls smile.

Not having a human heart, the wind was unaware of how such a sight would affect the woman.

The wind's naivety, though, was a kind that stemmed from the wish to make the woman happy and because of this it carried no sense of violation in relation to its actions, and felt no awareness of how such an attempt to replace her daughter would, of course, break the woman's heart.

The wind felt the birds arrive before it heard them; they fell through the sky like arrows, wings beating a vortex of air that rebuffed the wind as it moved the shaped tangle of leaves and branches towards the house.

The birds chattered in panic and darted back and forward and even through the winds puppet-girl, tearing away the twigs and leaves, snatching the grass and moss until nothing was left.

The wind was so surprised that it had no time to protect its creation. Why would the birds do such a thing, it wondered? Did they not know that the wind could give chase to them all and sweep them from the world?

As the wind ran its fingers over the stray branches and twigs dropped by the sparrows and crows, it became aware of something other than itself in the autumn air; a presence that seemed to now ebb away into the background of the world. The wind suddenly felt smaller than it could fully perceive, as if there were layers upon layers of minds like itself, invisible except for vague remnants of their actions and influence.

The wind did not understand the notion of taboo but it felt as if by trying to contact the woman in such a way that it had strayed beyond its allowed boundaries and this made the wind wonder, once again, just who it was.

The wind then rolled deeply inside itself, forming a tight cocoon around its mind and the image of the girl so that it would never forget her.

6.

The wind roamed the earth, uncaring and lost in a dream. Its external form became chaotic and unpredictable, sweeping snow into places of summer and humid monsoons upon the glassy, groaning backs of ancient icebergs, twisting the seasons and breaking the patterns of long fixed climates. And while the wind hid its mind away, the world was losing itself to war.

Blossoms of fire lit up the cities, and new diseases, carried by bombs that circled the entire Earth, crept across every continent. Sickness and famine settled into the burning ground, killing the fruits and fields, woodlands and all the rivers and oceans.

The wind, numbed by its grief for the girl, moved submissively on the magnesium white blasts and debris-filled currents of heat, unknowingly blistering the last birds and insects and the starving handfuls of human survivors who hid away in caves and in the basements of once shining towers that had become mere blackened, broken bones jutting into the charcoal sky. The wind never heard the last cries of the world, and, instead, listened only to the memory of its question to the girl.

"Whoo?" it whispered to itself, over and over as it hung above the dying Earth, "Whoo?"

7.

Time passed. The wind could not say how long because it had stopped counting the years when the centuries began to feel like seconds and when the eons became its days.

The world was no longer what it had once been. The age of man had passed and out of the scars of countless broken places new life formed. The wind had settled over the land where the girl had lived but sometimes it would observe from afar as the world brought forth a plant or flower that would thrive for a while. But eventually it would become extinct when its spores and seeds perished without the means to move to new ground.

As the world passed through ice ages and solar storms, meteor strikes and pole shifts, the wind watched as new life struggled and died over and over again.

The wind did not understand that it was its own refusal to comb and upturn the soil and it's unwillingness to carry the precious seeds of new creation which was holding the world back and which kept it in such a barren and dead state.

Instead, the wind was only intent on carrying its now ancient loss, and on mourning for the girl whose passing glimmered like the arriving light of a star long since burnt away.

And yet, it was the winds preoccupation with the girl that eventually ended the spell of its introspection.

A new flower, tiny and fragile, broke the skin of soil that had miraculously fostered its birth. Somehow, it had managed to perfume the air with its scent, reminding the wind of the Kadupul flower it had brought the girl, and the wind, its senses provoked, began to remember the world as it had once been.

The wind remembered the vibrant greens of tropical forests and the tumultuous explosions of great waterfalls whose ringing waters misted the surrounding rocks and banks, creating secret rainbows upon the winds back. It remembered the music of beating wings and bird-call and how it would laugh and carry the soft weight of young eagles upon its arms. It was connected then: a part of something more than itself, yet that needed its caress and response to survive. And, for the second time in the winds existence it felt the abstract presence of minds and purposes beyond its own.

So, the wind began to blow.

The work of the wind took many years. It dragged water from the seas to dry, desolate lands and unfurled itself from the sheltered places where new plants and flowers emerged, lifting them carefully from mountains and meadows then scattering their seeds all across the world.

The new Earth was unlike the planet the wind once knew. Strange, exotic, creatures filled the lands and oceans, and the wind watched in wonder as new eco-systems thrived and spread across the planet. Herds of fantastical creatures migrated through the borderless continents and roamed the flourishing plains. New birds took to the skies. Their feathers and fur combined with coloured bones that glittered like jewels as they propelled themselves through the air and drifted on the winds arms.

The world lived again.

8.

Time continued to pass and the wind watched life begin, thrive and end, over and over. The rise and fall of creatures and civilizations became like the beating of a heart; there, gone, there, gone. The wind lost count of how many types of new life the world brought forth but it still never forgot the girl.

Eventually, just as the lives upon the world rise and fall, so too do entire universes. The scales of these spans were beyond even the mind of the wind, but it could feel something change when the sun, at last, began its slow dying burnout.
It began with wave after wave of impossible heat scorching the planet. The wind watched in sorrow as all life eventually succumbed to the suns expansion until the world itself became engulfed in its reaching fire.

In its final moments, the wind became scared. Everything it had ever known was coming to an end, including itself.

When the world became ashes,
the wind,
at last,

stopped.

9.

The wind could not explain how it could see, but it was moving over a glistening white expanse. Faster and faster it ran, something rising within itself; a feeling it had once known but almost forgotten.

Out of the fog of whiteness something began to emerge: a house at the edge of a once remembered forest.

The wind descended slowly and moved towards the shape that sat waiting on the old swing. All around, the brightness shimmered.

The wind could not explain how it could see, but the girl was waiting.

She beckoned the wind closer and smiled as she reached out her hand.

And when she spoke, the wind finally knew its name.

ACKNOWLEDGEMENTS.

Many thanks to all of those who have been part of this book's long journey. I would like to thank my wife, Ciara, for all of her support. I am grateful to Paul Kilkenny, who offered valuable advice regarding the text itself.
I would like to acknowledge the support given to the manuscript by Maurice Joyce and Nuria G. Blanco with respect to visual imagery, in particular.
And, a huge thank you to John Jones for his wonderful interpretations of the scenes and story, and whose drawings compliment the writing so well.

David Halpin 2021.

www.ingramcontent.com/pod-product-compliance
Lightning Source LLC
Chambersburg PA
CBHW060618120726
48002CB00010B/3021